This igloo book belongs to:

_____

igloobooks

Published in 2013
by Igloo Books Ltd
Cottage Farm
Sywell
NN6 0BJ
www.igloobooks.com

FIR003 0313
2 4 6 8 10 9 7 5 3 1
ISBN 978-1-78197-291-5

Printed and manufactured in China

Party
Princess

igloobooks

Princess Posy was having breakfast with her mother, the queen. "I'm so excited," said Posy, stroking Cuddles, her cat. "There are only two days until my birthday. I can't wait to open my presents."

"Would you like to invite some of your friends over for a party?" asked the queen. "We can help you organize it." "Oh, yes, please, a party would be lovely," replied Posy. "I'd like to organize it myself, if you don't mind. After all, I'm a big girl now."

Posy found some invitations with the royal crest on and wrote each one out in her best handwriting. There was one for Princess Honey, another for Princess Bella and another for Princess Daisy. Posy carefully signed each invitation and Cuddles even added her paw print.

Princess Posy would like the pleasure of your company at her birthday party. It will be held in the Royal Gardens on Saturday at 3 o'clock.

Love from

Posy

and Cuddles

Please reply to:
Princess Posy
The Palace
Royal Walk
Castlewick Green

Posy held Cuddles up to the royal postbox and Cuddles delicately dropped the envelopes inside, one by one.
"I can't wait for my birthday party!" said Posy, happily.

That night, Princess Posy cuddled up in her bed.
She was very proud that she was organizing a party all by herself and she hoped that all her friends could come.

"We are going to have lots of fun," Posy said, stroking Cuddles who purred, happily. "I just wish we didn't have to wait for two whole days."

Posy imagined what dress she would wear, how delicious the party food would be and how happy she would feel. She drifted off to sleep and dreamed of balloons, birthday cake and lovely, ribbon-wrapped presents.

At last, the morning of Posy's birthday came. She jumped out of bed, pulled on her dress and dashed downstairs with Cuddles to see her mother and father.

"Happy Birthday, Posy!" cried the king and queen. They gave the princess a big hug and then handed her a box, wrapped in shiny paper and tied with a pink silk ribbon. "What is it?" asked Posy.

Her father and mother smiled. "Open it and see," they said, smiling. "We think you'll like it."

Posy pulled off the wrapping paper and opened the small box. Inside, was a shining, gold crown with tiny gems around the base. "Oh, it's beautiful, thank you," said Posy. She put on the crown and looked in the mirror. "Now I feel like a real princess," she said.

"I must get things ready for the party," Posy said and she ran outside, into the royal garden.

Posy put a tablecloth on a round table and set it neatly with cutlery, plates and glasses. She blew up balloons and tied bows onto the chairs. "Some flowers will finish it off nicely and then I'll be ready for my party," said Posy.

Cuddles thought that getting ready for the party was great fun. She tried to catch the ribbons as Posy was tying them into bows. Then, she wanted to play with the balloons. "Leave them alone, Cuddles," said Princess Posy, but Cuddles didn't listen. She got so excited when the balloons began to float off, she pounced on one and it went, BANG! "That will teach you," said Posy, laughing. "Come on it's time we iced my birthday cake."

In the palace kitchen, Posy put on an apron. She mixed a big bowl of icing sugar and carefully covered the cake. Posy decorated it with little hearts and flowers, then put candles on top.

Finally, she put a paper crown in the middle. "Doesn't it look lovely?" said Princess Posy, but Cuddles was far too busy licking the bowl of delicious, sweet icing sugar.

Soon, it was time for Princess Posy to put on her party dress. She opened the wardrobe in her bedroom and took out a lovely, swishy pink and purple dress with a golden bow. She put on her best party shoes and her star necklace and looked in the mirror.

Just then, Posy felt Cuddles tugging at her dress. "Oh, Cuddles, don't worry, you will have something nice to wear for the party, too," she said. Posy put a little crown on Cuddles' head and a bit of ribbon around her neck. "Now we are both ready," she said.

Just then, Posy heard a pitter-patter noise on her window pane. "Oh, no, it's raining!" she cried.

Outside, the rain began to fall faster and faster. Balloons came loose and the tablecloth flapped in the wind.

Posy picked up Cuddles and held her. They looked out of the window and watched as the beautifully set party table was soaked by the storm.

Soon, balloons began to pop and the glasses filled with rainwater. "Oh, dear," said Posy sadly, giving Cuddles a squeeze. "Everything is ruined. Now I won't be able to have my party after all."

Cuddles miaowed softly as Princess Posy began to cry.

Posy ran downstairs to her mother and father. "Don't worry," said the king, "you can't let a bit of rain spoil the fun. Come on, we'll help you to put things right."

The queen went off to get another tablecloth and some more cutlery. "We'll set a table in the dining room," she said, "it will be nice and cozy in there."

Princess Posy set the table and the king blew up lots of balloons. "This is the most fun I've had in years!" he said.

The queen made some streamers and bows and before anyone knew it, everything was finished. "Thank you so much," said Posy, hugging her parents. "It looks perfect. I'm glad you were here to help me."

Just then, the palace doorbell rang. The guests had arrived. "Happy Birthday, Posy!" they cried as they came in with their presents.

Princess Honey gave Posy a new storybook. Princess Bella gave her a photo frame and Princess Daisy gave her a lovely box with a star on top.

"Thank you so much for my lovely presents," said Posy.
The friends chatted happily as they ate the delicous party food and
drank homemade lemonade, then Posy blew out her candles.

Princess Posy and her friends played party games all afternoon. Everyone had lots of fun, especially Cuddles.

Later on, after lots more birthday cake, it was time to go home. "Thank you for coming," said Posy as she waved goodbye to her friends and closed the palace door.

Posy gave her parents a big hug and went upstairs. She was very tired after all the excitement, but before going to bed, she wrote a thank-you note to each of her friends, starting with Princess Honey.

When she had finished, Posy put away her pen and paper and got ready for bed. "I'm so tired," she said stretching and yawning. Cuddles gave a soft little, "Miaow," and lay down.

Dear Princess Honey,

Thank you very much for the wonderful storybook you gave me. I am really looking forward to reading it before bedtime. I hope you enjoyed the party and I can't wait until the next one.

See you soon,
Love Posy xxx

Soon, Posy snuggled down in bed. The king and queen said goodnight and made sure that she was tucked up tight.

As she closed her eyes, Princess Posy remembered that she hadn't made a wish when she blew out the candles on her birthday cake. "I wish that next year will be as good as this," she said. "Then I really will be the perfect party princess."